1 one

two 2

3 three

4 four

RESTROOM

six 6

5 five

seven 7

ten 10

9

8 eight

nine

sixteen 16

17

seventeen

11 eleven

12 twelve

13 thirteen

14 fourteen

15 fifteen

18 eighteen

19 nineteen

20 twenty

Counting Our Way to Maine

A MELANIE KROUPA BOOK

Orchard Books, A Grolier Company
95 Madison Avenue, New York, NY 10016

Manufactured in the United States of America. Printed and bound by Phoenix Color Corp.
Book design by Sylvia Frezzolini Severance. The text of this book is set in 20 point Goudy.
The illustrations are watercolor, gouache, and pastel with ink and pencil line.

Hardcover 10 9 8 7 6 5 4 3
Paperback 10 9 8 7 6 5 4 3 2

Library of Congress Cataloging-in-Publication Data
Smith, Maggie, date. Counting our way to Maine / Maggie Smith.   p.   cm.
"A Melanie Kroupa book"—Half t.p.
Summary: On a trip to Maine, the family counts from one baby to twenty fireflies.
ISBN 0-531-06884-6 (tr.) — ISBN 0-531-08734-4 (lib. bdg.) ISBN 0-531-07117-0 (pbk.)
[1. Voyages and travels—Fiction. 2. Counting.] I. Title.
PZ7.S65474Co 1995 [E]—dc20 94-24874

Counting Our Way to Maine

Maggie Smith

ORCHARD BOOKS   NEW YORK

for Mom & Dad

1 For our trip to Maine this summer
we packed one baby,

2 two dogs,

3 and three bicycles.

4 As we left the city behind us,
we passed four taxicabs

5 and five smokestacks.

6 We had to stop for the bathroom six times!

7 When we were halfway there, we stopped again and ate seven ice creams.

8 Then we climbed into the car and drove over and around eight mountains.

9 Before long we had to stop again.
Nine deer watched us.

10 When we finally arrived at the cottage, there were ten slugs waiting on the steps!

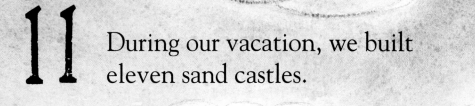

11

During our vacation, we built eleven sand castles.

12 We went down to the dock and saw twelve lobster pots

13

and thirteen boats.

14

As the fog lifted, we spotted fourteen buoys bobbing on the waves.

15 One hot day we climbed a steep hill and filled fifteen boxes with blueberries.

16 And the next day we made
sixteen blueberry pies.

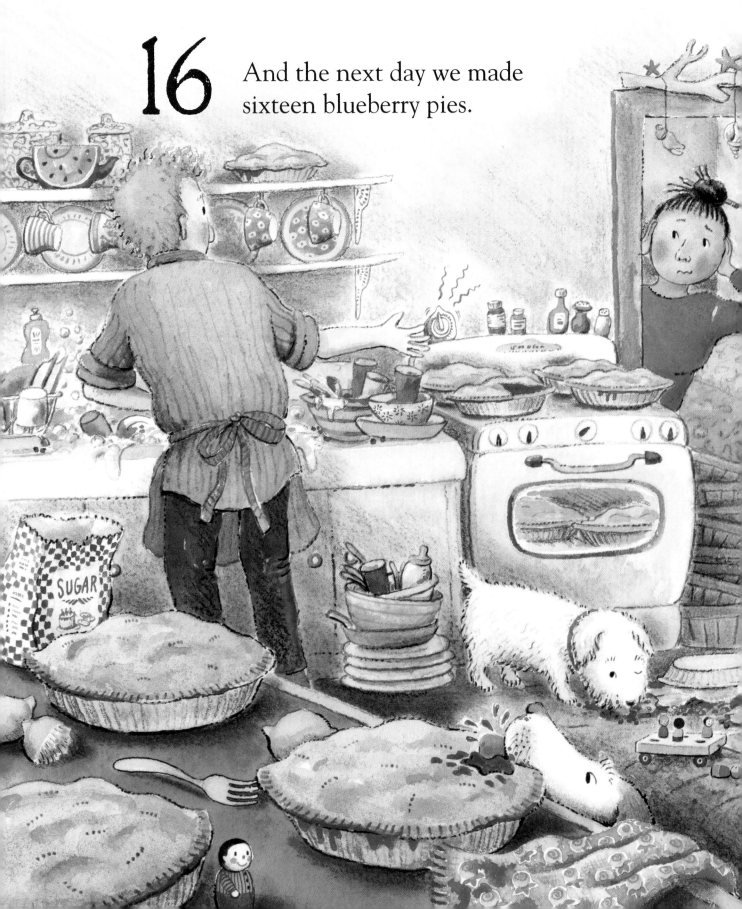

17 We went into the woods early one morning and found seventeen mushrooms.

18

When we got back to the cottage, we counted eighteen mosquito bites!

19 For our cookout the last night we went to a nearby cove and dug nineteen clams.

20

That evening, as the tide crept in to say good-bye

we chased twenty fireflies

The next morning we let our fireflies go.

And for our trip back to the city
we packed one baby . . .

11 eleven

12 twelve

13 thirteen

14 fourteen

15 fifteen

18 eighteen

19 nineteen

20 twenty